pay back

By Eleanor Robins

D0735524

SADDLEBACK
EDUCATIONAL PUBLISHING

SADDLEBACK
EDUCATIONAL PUBLISHING
www.sdlback.com

ISBN-13: 978-1-61651-594-2
ISBN-10: 1-61651-594-5
eBook: 978-1-61247-240-9

Printed in Malaysia

21 20 19 18 17   6 7 8 9 10

Meet the Characters from

pay back

Brad: dates Rae, finds out the truth

Rae: dates Chance—or used to, dates Brad, is Jess's best friend

Rae's Dad: drives Rae and her friends around

Chance: dates Torie, used to date Rae

Torie: dates Chance, likes Brad

chapter

1

Rae walked down the hall at school. She was on her way to class. Then she saw Jess. Jess was her best friend.

Rae wanted to talk to Jess. So she hurried to meet her.

Rae yelled, "Jess, wait for me!"

Rae looked very mad. And she sounded very mad, too.

Jess stopped and waited for Rae. "You look mad, Rae. What's wrong?" Jess asked.

Rae hissed, "You'd better believe I'm

mad. I'll pay her back. I promise!"

"Why are you so upset, Rae? And who do you want to pay back?" Jess asked.

"Torie," Rae said. Torie was in her science class. Rae didn't like Torie.

"What did Torie do?" Jess asked.

"She had a date with Chance last Friday night. I just found out about it," Rae said.

Rae and Chance had gone on a few dates. And Rae liked him a lot.

Jess said, "Calm down, Rae. It isn't a big deal."

"It is to me. I like Chance," Rae said.

Jess said, "Don't worry about it. Torie likes Brad. So I don't think she'll date Chance for long."

"I don't care. She shouldn't have dated Chance at all," Rae said.

Rae still looked mad.

Jess said, "Rae, Torie really likes

Brad, not Chance. So you are getting upset about nothing."

"I'm not upset about nothing. And I'll pay Torie back," Rae said.

"Forget about it, Rae. It's no big deal," Jess said again.

"It is to me. Just you wait and see," Rae said.

Jess looked worried. "What are you going to do, Rae?" she asked.

"Torie likes Brad. I'll get Brad to ask me out on a date. And that will pay Torie back," Rae said.

"You don't even like Brad. You've never wanted to date him before. So why do you want to date him now?" Jess asked.

Jess was right about that. Rae didn't like Brad. And she'd never wanted to date him before.

"I just told you why I want to date

Brad. I want to pay Torie back. She dated Chance. And I have to get even with her," Rae said.

"Forget about it, Rae," Jess said.

Rae said, "I don't care what you think, Jess. I'll get Brad to ask me out."

"Don't do it, Rae. You don't even like Brad," Jess said.

"So what? I just want to date him," Rae said. "I don't want to *marry* him," Rae said.

"But it wouldn't be fair to get Brad to date you. You wouldn't want a guy to date you to get even with another girl. Think of how that would make you feel. And Brad would feel that way, too," Jess said.

"He won't know the reason why I want to date him," Rae said.

"But someone might tell him," Jess said.

"You're the only person who knows. And you won't tell him, will you?" Rae asked.

"No. But he could still find out," Jess said.

"No way. Only two of us would know. You are my best friend. You won't tell him. And I sure won't," Rae said.

"Don't do it, Rae. Think about it some more. Think about how you would feel," Jess said.

"Don't try to make me feel bad, Jess. I'll get a date with Brad. And I'll pay Torie back. Just you wait and see," Rae said.

chapter 2

Rae hurried into the lunchroom. She got her lunch. Then she looked for Jess.

Rae saw Jess sitting at a table. Rae hurried over to the table. And she quickly sat down. Rae looked at Jess.

"I have a plan. And I can't wait to tell you about it," Rae blurted.

"What kind of plan?" Jess asked.

"A plan to get Brad to ask me out on a date," Rae said. She had a big smile on her face.

Jess said, "Forget about Brad. And

forget about your plan, Rae." Jess looked worried again.

"No way, Jess. Don't you want to hear my plan?" Rae asked.

Jess said, "Not really. But I guess you'll tell me anyway."

"I found out Brad will be at the pep rally tonight," Rae said. The school had a football game the next night. And the school always had a pep rally the night before.

Rae said, "Brad is going by himself. And I'll go without a date, too." She laughed. "I'll get my dad to take me. That's the first part of my plan."

"Do you want me to go with you?" Jess asked.

"You can ride to the pep rally with me. But we can't stay together once we get there. You'll have to find your own way home," Rae said.

Jess asked, "Why? Did your dad say he couldn't come back and get you?"

"No," Rae said. She laughed again.

"Then why would I need to find my own way home? Is there a reason why I can't ride home with you?" Jess asked.

Rae said, "Yes. I told my dad that I didn't want him to come back for me."

Jess looked surprised. "Why did you tell your dad that?" Jess asked.

"I told you. I have a plan," Rae said.

"So what's your plan?" Jess asked.

"I'll look for Brad at the pep rally. Then I'll get him to take me home," Rae said.

"A lot of people will be at the pep rally, Rae. You might not see him," Jess said.

"Don't worry about that. I'll find Brad. You can count on that," Rae said.

"Maybe. But you can't be sure that he'll take you home," Jess said.

"Maybe not. But I can always make another plan," Rae said.

Jess looked worried. She picked up her milk carton and drank some of her milk.

Then Jess said, "I wish you would forget about dating Brad."

"No way. I told you that I'll pay Torie back. And I will," Rae said.

Jess said, "Just forget about it, Rae. You haven't dated Chance in more than a month. So why do you care?"

"I still want to date him," Rae said.

And that was true. She did want to date Chance.

Jess said, "But Torie doesn't know that, Rae. So you can't blame her for dating Chance."

"She knows that Chance is my boyfriend, Jess," Rae said.

Jess said, "But that's just it, Rae.

Chance hasn't asked you out on a date in a month. So I don't think you can say that he's your boyfriend."

"I don't care how long it's been since we dated. He's still my boyfriend. And I'll pay Torie back," Rae said.

chapter

3

Later that night, Rae and her dad sat in her dad's car. Jess was with them. They were on their way to the pep rally.

Rae's dad stopped the car in front of the school gym. He said, "I can come back for you, Rae. Are you sure you don't want me to?"

"Yes, Dad. I'm sure. I hope to get a ride home. But I'll call you if I don't," Rae said.

"Okay," her dad said.

Rae opened the car door on her side

of the car. She got out. Then Rae looked back at her dad. She said, "Bye, Dad." Then she closed the door.

Jess opened the car door on her side of the car. She got out. She said, "Thanks for the ride." Then she closed her door.

Rae's dad said, "Have fun, girls. And be sure to call if you need a ride." Then he drove off.

Rae looked around the parking lot. She saw Brad's car. "I see Brad's car. So he's here for sure," Rae said.

"But he might have brought someone with him," Jess said.

"Maybe. But I don't think he did. I heard that he would come by himself," Rae said.

The two girls hurried into the gym. A lot of students were already there.

"Be sure to find a ride, Jess," Rae said.

"I will," Jess said.

Rae said, "I need to look for Brad. So I can't sit with you. I'll call you after I get home."

"Okay," Jess said.

Rae hurried off. She started to walk around the gym. She spoke to everyone who spoke to her. But she didn't stop to talk.

Rae could ask someone where she might find Brad. But she didn't want anyone to know that she was looking for him.

Rae walked around the gym for about ten minutes. Then she saw Brad. He sat in the bleachers with some students from her math class.

Rae climbed up the bleachers to where he sat.

She said, "Hi, Brad. This looks like a good place to sit. You can see really well from here. Is it okay if I sit here?"

"Sure," Brad said. He moved over so Rae could sit down. And Rae sat down next to him.

For a few minutes Rae didn't talk. She hoped that Brad would say something to her. But he didn't. Then Rae said, "I sure hope we win the game tomorrow."

"Yeah. Me, too," Brad said.

The other students started to cheer. Rae and Brad yelled some cheers with them. Then they all stopped cheering. Rae looked at Brad.

She said, "This is a great pep rally."

"Yeah. It is," Brad said.

"I'm having such a great time. I don't want this pep rally to end," Rae said.

"Yeah. Me either," Brad said.

But Rae knew the pep rally would end soon. And she wanted Brad to take her home. So it was time to hint to him that she needed a ride. Just maybe he would offer to take her home.

"How did you get here tonight, Brad?" she asked.

Rae knew how Brad got there. He drove his car. She'd seen it in the parking lot.

"I drove my car," Brad said.

Rae said, "My dad drove me to the pep rally. But he can't come back for me. I sure hope I can find a ride home."

"Do you want me to give you a ride home?" Brad asked.

"Oh, would you, Brad? That would be so nice of you," Rae purred.

Brad said, "Sure. It isn't a big deal. I go by your house on my way home."

Rae was very happy. She did it! She got Brad to offer her a ride home.

Soon the pep rally was over. Rae and Brad walked out of the gym. They started to walk to his car.

Rae saw Torie. Torie looked straight at them. And she seemed very upset. .

Rae did it! She had paid Torie back. Rae was very happy about that.

chapter 4

The next morning, Rae's dad drove Rae to school. Most of the time she rode the bus to school. But today she wanted to get there early. She wanted to talk to Jess before school started. Rae asked her dad to drive her there.

Rae and her dad got to the school. Her dad stopped in the front. Rae opened her door.

She said, "Thanks for the ride, Dad."

"See you tonight, Rae. Have a good day," her dad said.

Rae quickly got out of the car and closed the door. Rae looked for Jess. At first she didn't see Jess. Then Jess yelled to her.

Jess said, "Rae, I'm over here."

Rae saw Jess. She waved at Rae. Rae hurried over to her.

Jess said, "You look very happy this morning."

"I am. I did it! I got Brad to take me home," Rae said.

"I know. I saw you leave the pep rally with him," Jess said.

Rae had a big smile on her face. She said, "And Torie saw us leave together. You should have seen how upset she looked."

Rae laughed. But Jess didn't laugh.

Jess said, "I still think you aren't being fair to Brad."

"You're wrong about that," Rae said.

Jess said, "Maybe. But I don't think so. And I think you should stop trying to pay Torie back."

"No way," Rae said. For a few minutes the two girls didn't talk.

Then Jess said, "You said you would call me last night, Rae. So why didn't you call me after you got home? You said that you would."

"I know I did. But I asked Brad if he wanted to stay for a while. He surprised me and said that he did. So he stayed," Rae said.

"How long did he stay?" Jess asked.

Rae said, "About an hour. It was too late to call you after he left."

"You could have texted. What did the two of you do?" Jess asked.

"We talked. And guess what Brad asked me," Rae said with big smile on her face.

"What?" Jess asked.

"He asked me to go to the game with him tonight. And I said *yes*," Rae gushed.

"Why doesn't that surprise me?" Jess said.

Rae laughed. Then she said, "I'll have so much fun there. I can't wait to see Torie's face when she sees us. That will pay her back *big* time."

Jess frowned at Rae.

Rae said, "Don't frown at me, Jess. I know you don't think I should go with Brad. It's only a date."

Jess said, "Brad might start to like you. And then what?"

"Don't worry about it, Jess. I plan to date Brad only a few times. Then I'll stop dating him. Torie can have him back."

"But Brad might start to like you," Jess said.

Rae said, "It will only be a few dates. Brad won't fall in love with me in just a few dates."

"You can't be sure about that, Rae. He might," Jess said.

"No way," Rae said.

"But some people fall in love quickly, Rae," Jess said.

"Not me," Rae said.

chapter 5

That night Rae sat with Brad in his car. They were on their way to the football game.

"Do you think we'll win tonight, Rae?" Brad asked.

"Sure. We'd better win. I don't like to lose," Rae said.

Rae laughed. Brad laughed, too. They talked about the game some more. And it wasn't long before they got to the football stadium.

Brad parked his car in the parking

lot. He quickly got out and closed the door. Then he walked around to Rae's door. Brad opened the door for Rae.

Rae got out of the car and Brad closed her door. Brad said, "We need to hurry. It won't be long until the game starts."

They quickly walked to a ticket booth. Brad bought two tickets. He gave one to Rae.

A person near the ticket booth was selling football programs. Brad said, "I want a program. Do you want one, too?"

"Yes. Thanks," Rae said. Rae was surprised Brad asked her about a program. Most guys bought just one. And they kept it.

Brad bought two programs. He gave one of them to Rae.

"Thanks," Rae said. They walked over to a gate. Two boys were taking up tickets at the gate. Rae and Brad gave their tickets to one of the boys.

Then they went to find seats. "Where do you want to sit?" Brad asked.

"Anywhere you want to sit," Rae said. Rae thought it was very nice of Brad to ask her that. Some guys just sat where they wanted to. They didn't ask her where she wanted to sit.

Rae didn't care where they sat. She just wanted Torie to see them.

Brad saw some good seats on the forty yard line. "Those seats up there okay?" he asked.

"Yes," Rae said.

They quickly climbed up the bleachers to the seats. Then they sat down. It wasn't long before the game started. Rae and Brad kept jumping up and down. They cheered and cheered some more.

Most of the time their team was ahead.

"What a game," Brad said.

"Yes. What a game," Rae said.

It was the last quarter. Their team was ahead by a touchdown. But their kicker had missed the extra point.

Only a few seconds were left when the other team scored.

Brad said, "I don't want to lose this game. Their kicker has to miss the extra point."

"I sure hope he does," Rae said.

But then the kicker made the extra point. And the other team led by one point. Suddenly the game ended.

Rae and Brad started to walk to Brad's car.

Rae was sure Brad would be in a bad mood. Most guys would be angry after they lost a game by one point.

"It's too bad we lost," Rae said.

"Yeah. But we can't win all of our

games. We'll win next time," Brad said.

Brad was a super nice guy. He wasn't at all like Rae thought he would be. And she hoped Brad would ask her for another date.

She didn't know if Torie had seen them at the game. And she didn't care. Rae no longer wanted to pay Torie back.

chapter 6

It was two weeks later. Rae hurried into the lunchroom. She had a big smile on her face.

Rae quickly got her lunch. She looked for Jess. Jess was sitting at a table. Jess waved to her. Rae hurried over to the table and sat down.

Jess asked, "Why do you look so happy, Rae?"

"I'm very happy. And you won't believe why," Rae said.

"Chance asked you for date," Jess said.

Rae said, "No. He didn't. And I don't want Chance to ask me for a date anymore."

Jess looked surprised. She asked, "Since when? For weeks all you've wanted is for Chance to ask you out on a date."

"I know. But things have changed," Rae said.

"What things? And how have they changed?" Jess asked.

"I'm in love," Rae said.

"So what's new? You've been in love with Chance for months. Or at least you thought you were," Jess said.

Rae said, "I just thought I was. But now I really *am* in love. I've never really been in love before. I know that now."

"So who's the guy?" Jess asked.

"Brad," Rae said.

Jess looked very surprised.

"Brad? You must be joking, Rae. You're

just dating him to make Torie jealous. You don't even like him," Jess said.

"I didn't like him before I started to date him. But Brad isn't like the other guys. He's nice and sweet. I really am in love this time," Rae said.

Jess laughed.

"It's not funny. I really do love him," Rae said.

"How many times does this make it that you have fallen in love? Four? Five? Or more?" Jess asked.

Jess picked up her milk carton. Then she drank some of her milk.

Rae said, "I've told you that I was in love before. So I know you don't believe me. But this isn't the same as before. I really do love Brad."

Jess put her milk carton back on the table. Then she looked at Rae.

"How can you be in love with Brad?

You dated him only to make Torie jealous. Not because you really liked him," Jess said.

"I know. But I'm in love with him now. He's the only guy I want to date," Rae said.

"Does Brad think he's in love with you?" Jess asked.

"I don't know. But I think he likes me a lot," Rae said.

Jess thought for a moment. Then she said, "You might be right, Rae. You might really be in love this time. But you have said you were in love before. And you might change your mind about Brad in a few weeks."

"No. I won't. This love is real. I hope you'll be happy for me," Rae said.

"Sure I am. You're my best friend. And I want you to be happy. But—," Jess said.

"But what?" Rae asked.

"I hope Brad doesn't find out why you really started dating him. That it was only to make Torie jealous," Jess said.

"But how could he find out? You are the only one who knows. And you won't tell him. It's our secret," Rae said.

Jess said, "No. I won't tell him. But sometimes other people find out secrets. Even when you think there's no way they can."

"There's no way Brad will find out. I'm sure about that," Rae said.

But all of a sudden Rae wasn't so sure.

How could Brad find out? Only Rae and Jess knew the truth.

chapter 7

Three days later, Rae stood at her locker. Jess was with her.

Torie stood at her locker, too. It was near Rae's locker.

Rae and Jess were talking to each other. But they weren't talking to Torie.

Rae said, "I had a really great time last night. It's so much fun to date Brad. I like him so much."

Torie slammed her locker shut. Then she walked over to Rae and Jess.

She looked at Rae. Torie looked very mad.

Torie said, "You think you're so smart, Rae. But I know the real reason why you're dating Brad. And it isn't because you *like* him."

Rae slammed her locker shut. Then she looked at Torie.

"What do you mean by that?" Rae hissed. She looked very mad.

"I know why you're dating Brad. And it isn't because you like him," Torie said again.

Torie spoke very loudly. The other students in the hall could hear her, too.

Jess said, "I don't think you should talk about this now. We need to go to class. We'll be late."

Torie said, "We won't be late. But I don't care if we are."

Torie spoke even louder. More and

more students in the hall looked at her.

Torie said, "You don't care about Brad, Rae. You're just dating him to upset me and make me jealous."

"That isn't true. I *do* like him," Rae shouted so that everyone could hear.

Jess said, "Come on, Rae. We need to go to class. And we need to go *now*."

Torie said, "Tell me the truth, Rae. You're dating Brad just to make me jealous. You know I like him. And because you like Chance, and I dated him…"

Rae was upset. She didn't stop to think about what she was saying.

Rae blurted, "That might be why I dated Brad the first two times. But that isn't true now. I like Brad. I like him a lot!"

Mrs. Drake hurried out of her classroom. She was Rae's math teacher.

"Girls, you need to go to class," Mrs. Drake said.

She then looked at all of the students who had stopped to listen to Rae and Torie.

"All of you should go to class, too," said Mrs. Drake.

The other students walked away quickly.

Torie said, "I knew I was right, Rae. I knew you dated Brad only to make me jealous. Thanks for telling me the truth."

Mrs. Drake said, "To your class, girls. *Now*."

Torie started to walk away. She had a big smile on her face.

"See you at lunch, Rae," Jess said.

Jess started to walk away, too. She didn't smile. Jess had a worried look on her face.

Rae started to walk slowly down the hall. She didn't feel well.

Why had she let Torie make her mad? So mad that she told Torie the truth?

Now Rae was very upset. She was sure Torie would tell Brad what she had said, or someone else would tell him.

Would Brad forgive her for what she'd done? Would he believe that she really liked him now?

chapter 8

Later that day, Rae walked slowly on her way to lunch. She looked for Brad. But she didn't see him.

Rae hoped she could tell Brad the truth before someone else did. But she knew that this type of news could travel very fast. Rae feared that Brad might already know.

She heard Brad's voice. He said, "Rae. Wait up for me."

Brad didn't sound mad. So maybe no one had told him yet.

Rae turned around. Then she saw Brad's face. He looked very mad. And she knew it was too late.

Brad quickly walked up to Rae.

"I thought you were a real sweet girl, Rae. And I thought you liked me a lot," Brad said. "But was I ever wrong. You don't care about me at all. You just wanted to make Torie jealous."

"That isn't true," Rae said. She had to make Brad believe that she really cared about him.

"Don't lie to me, Rae. Torie said she got you to tell her the truth. That you dated me only to make her jealous. You might lie to me. But Torie always tells me the truth," Brad said.

"Brad, please let me explain," Rae said.

"There isn't anything to explain. You

dated me only to make Torie jealous,"
Brad said.

"Yes, I did that the first two times we went out. But not after that. I like you, Brad. I like you a lot. Please believe me," Rae said.

"Believe you? You must be joking. I'll never again believe anything you say," Brad said. He started to walk away.

"Please call me after school, Brad. Or come to my house. We can talk," Rae said.

Brad stopped and turned around. He said, "No, Rae. I don't ever want to talk to you again."

Brad turned and quickly walked down the hall.

"Brad, please come back," Rae yelled after him. But Brad didn't look back.

Rae watched Brad until he walked

out the door. She felt a few tears slide slowly down her face. She quickly wiped them away with her hand.

A crowd of students had seen the whole thing. But she didn't care. Rae had lost Brad. And it was all her fault.

Rae hurried to the lunchroom. She needed to talk to Jess. She looked for Jess. Jess sat at a table. And she waved to Rae. Rae hurried over to the table and sat down.

Jess said, "Brad found out. Didn't he? I can tell from the look on your face. Who told him? Torie?"

"Yes," Rae said. A few more tears slid slowly down her face. She wiped them away with her hand.

"What did Brad say? Do you think he'll forgive you?" Jess asked.

Rae said, "No. He doesn't want to talk to me."

"I'm so sorry, Rae. I really am," Jess said.

"You told me that I shouldn't pay Torie back. And I didn't listen to you. But now it's too late. I've lost Brad," Rae said.

Then Jess said, "Maybe Brad will change his mind, Rae. Maybe he'll date you again."

"He won't. I've lost him. It's all my fault," Rae said.

Jess didn't say anything. Rae knew that Jess thought that it was her fault, too.

Rae said, "I did pay Torie back for dating Chance. But I got paid back much worse!"

consider
this...

1. Is getting even, or paying someone back, ever a good idea? Why or why not?

2. What should you do when you know that a friend is about to make a big mistake?

3. What do Brad's actions tell you about him?

4. Why does Jess think that Rae should consider how Brad feels about her?

5. Why doesn't Jess believe Rae when she tells her that she loves Brad?